D0717849

OXFORD
UNIVERSITY PRESS

Great Clarendon Street, Oxford OX2 6DP

Oxford University Press is a department of the University of Oxford.
It furthers the University's objective of excellence in research, scholarship,
and education by publishing worldwide in

Oxford   New York

Auckland   Cape Town   Dar es Salaam   Hong Kong   Karachi
Kuala Lumpur   Madrid   Melbourne   Mexico City   Nairobi
New Delhi   Shanghai   Taipei   Toronto

With offices in

Argentina   Austria   Brazil   Chile   Czech Republic   France   Greece
Guatemala   Hungary   Italy   Japan   Poland   Portugal   Singapore
South Korea   Switzerland   Thailand   Turkey   Ukraine   Vietnam

Oxford is a registered trade mark of Oxford University Press
in the UK and in certain other countries

© Ian Beck 1998, 2005

The moral rights of the author have been asserted

Database right Oxford University Press (maker)

First published 2005
Reissued with a new cover 2007
This edition published 2010

All rights reserved. No part of this publication may be reproduced,
stored in a retrieval system, or transmitted, in any form or by any means,
without the prior permission in writing of Oxford University Press,
or as expressly permitted by law, or under terms agreed with the appropriate
reprographics rights organization. Enquiries concerning reproduction
outside the scope of the above should be sent to the Rights Department,
Oxford University Press, at the address above

You must not circulate this book in any other binding or cover
and you must impose this same condition on any acquirer

British Library Cataloguing in Publication Data

Data available

ISBN-13: 978-0-19-279294-5 (paperback)

1 3 5 7 9 10 8 6 4 2

Printed in China

Paper used in the production of this book is a natural,
recyclable product made from wood grown in sustainable forests
The manufacturing process conforms to the environmental
regulations of the country of origin

The ELVES and the SHOEMAKER

IAN BECK

OXFORD
UNIVERSITY PRESS

Once upon a time, when the world was young and snow fell every winter, there lived a shoemaker and his wife. He was a fine craftsman, but recently trade had not been good, and they were very poor. The time came when the shoemaker had only one piece of leather left – enough to make just one pair of shoes. So, that evening, he sat in his cold workshop and cut out the leather into all the shapes he needed for the shoes.

Then his wife called him in for their supper,
and so he wearily left all the cut-out pieces on
the bench ready to make up in the morning.

After a poor supper of watery cabbage soup
and scraps, the shoemaker and his wife lit
their last candle and made their way to bed.

When the shoemaker opened his workshop door in the morning he had the shock of his life. There on the bench stood the finest pair of shoes he had ever seen. He looked around for the pieces of leather but everything was tidy as always. Then he called to his wife to come, and together they peered closely at the shoes. It was his leather all right but the stitches were tiny and neat.

'Made by a master hand, much finer than my own,' he said. 'But where did they come from?'

'No matter,' said his wife. 'Let us be glad. These shoes will make our fortune, you'll see.' And she put the shoes in the middle of the shop window.

It was not long before the shoes were noticed. A gentleman came in and tried them on. Walking up and down the shop, he said they were the most comfortable and handsome shoes he had ever worn, and he happily paid twice the normal price for them.

Now there was enough money to buy leather to make two pairs of shoes, and even some left over for a good supper.

That evening the shoemaker cut out the leather and left the pieces ready for making up in the morning; and that night the soup was thicker and tastier, and the shoemaker and his wife went to bed well satisfied.

And sure enough, in the morning, when the shoemaker opened his workshop, there were two pairs of perfectly made shoes, all complete with their tiny stitching, and the leather soft and glossy with polish.

The shoes were soon sold, and the shoemaker was able to buy enough leather to make four pairs of shoes. Again the shoemaker carefully cut out the patterns, and again in the morning there stood four more pairs of exquisite shoes, and so it went on.

The shoemaker was able to buy more and more leather in all the colours of the rainbow.

He cut out pieces for a great variety of shoes, and pumps, and slippers, and boots. Every morning he would come in to find them all perfectly finished as before.

He was soon thought to be the best shoemaker in the land, and one morning the king himself arrived with his page and chancellor and bought an especially fine pair of high boots in green leather.

One night the shoemaker and his wife decided to hide themselves in the workshop to see who it was at work. They left a tall candle on the workbench, and then settled in their hiding place to wait.

When the clock chimed midnight a pair of strange little figures climbed up on to the workbench. They were tiny, not much bigger than a shoe themselves, and they wore very

odd clothes: acorn halves for hats, leaves and grasses and scraps for clothes. 'Elves,' gasped the shoemaker.

The elves worked hard and fast. They stitched with tiny needles, and hammered with tiny hammers, and buffed and polished with little cloths.

They worked all through the night and didn't stop until the candle was almost burnt down and daylight showed through the frosty window. Then the two elves scuttled back under the door, leaving a line of beautiful shoes on the bench.

The shoemaker and his wife crept out of their hiding place.

'Did you ever see anything like it?' said the shoemaker. 'Those elves have helped us to make our fortune. And did you see what they were wearing? Just little scraps, and acorns, and bits and bobs. They must be frozen in this weather.' And the shoemaker and his wife shook their heads.

'I have an idea,' said the shoemaker's wife. 'We shall make some fine clothes for them, as a way of saying thank you.'

So, during the day (which was Christmas Eve), the shoemaker and his wife cut and sewed with their nimble fingers.

They made some little shirts, and waistcoats, and jackets, and breeches, and even stockings and mittens. They used pieces of brocade, velvet, silk, cambric, and fine wool.

That night they laid out all the little
clothes on the workbench, and again settled
themselves in their hiding place to wait.

Sure enough, as the clock chimed midnight
the two elves appeared. They climbed up to
the workbench, where they found all the fine

new clothes, beautifully cut and sewn. The elves put on their new clothes, laughing and chattering to themselves.

'Happy Christmas, little men,' whispered the shoemaker and his wife.

Then the elves danced round the candlestick, and as they danced they sang,

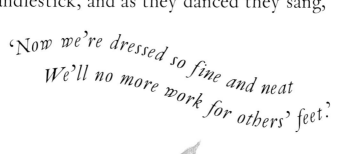

'Now we're dressed so fine and neat
We'll no more work for others' feet.'

And then they danced off the bench, under the door, and were never seen again.

The shoemaker and his wife hung a smart new sign on the front of their shop; it was cut out in the shape of an elegant shoe, and there was a crown to show that even the king was one of their customers.

The shoemaker and his wife lived happily and prospered until the end of their days, which was a very long time indeed.

I0653228

LIVE
LAUGH
LOVE

summersdale

LIVE, LAUGH, LOVE

This edition copyright © Summersdale Publishers Ltd, 2017

First published in 2014

Geometric pattern © elyomys/Shutterstock.com

Research by Sarah Viner

All rights reserved.

No part of this book may be reproduced by any means, nor transmitted, nor translated into a machine language, without the written permission of the publishers.

Condition of Sale
This book is sold subject to the condition that it shall not, by way of trade or otherwise, be lent, resold, hired out or otherwise circulated in any form of binding or cover other than that in which it is published and without a similar condition including this condition being imposed on the subsequent purchaser.

Summersdale Publishers Ltd
46 West Street
Chichester
West Sussex
PO19 1RP
UK

www.summersdale.com

Printed and bound in India

ISBN: 978-1-78685-027-0

Substantial discounts on bulk quantities of Summersdale books are available to corporations, professional associations and other organisations. For details contact general enquiries: telephone: +44 (0) 1243 771107 or email: enquiries@summersdale.com.

To...

From.......................................

One cannot
have too large
a party.

Jane Austen

LAUGHTER IS AN INSTANT VACATION.

Milton Berle

All the statistics in the world can't measure the warmth of a smile.

Chris Hart

Plunge boldly into the thick of life, and seize it where you will.

Johann Wolfgang von Goethe

Love is being stupid together.

Paul Valéry

Mix a little foolishness with your serious plans. It is lovely to be silly at the right moment.

Horace

Dare to love yourself as if you were a rainbow with gold at both ends.

Aberjhani

Laughter is the sound of the soul dancing.

Jarod Kintz

Too much of
a ~~good thing~~ can
be wonderful.

Mae West

**Every day brings
a chance for you
to draw in a breath,
kick off your shoes...
and dance.**

Oprah Winfrey

DON'T GO THROUGH LIFE, ~~GROW~~ THROUGH LIFE.

Eric Butterworth

Life is a great
big canvas, and you
should throw all
the paint on
it you can.

Danny Kaye

Laughter is
the brush that
sweeps away
the cobwebs
of your heart.

Mort Walker

Opportunities don't often come along. So, when they do, you have to grab them.

Audrey Hepburn

**Where there
is great love,
there are always
miracles.**

Willa Cather

Laughter is a tranquiliser with no side effects.

Arnold H. Glasow

LOVE ALL,
TRUST
A FEW,
DO WRONG
TO NONE.

William Shakespeare

Find something you're passionate about and keep tremendously interested in it.

Julia Child

The good life is
one inspired by
love and guided
by knowledge.

Bertrand Russell

IF YOU GIVE PEOPLE A CHANCE, THEY SHINE.

Billy Connolly

Whoever is happy will make others happy too.

Anne Frank

There is little success where there is little laughter.

Andrew Carnegie

It's more fun to
be the painter
than the paint.

George Clooney

WHERE THERE IS LOVE THERE IS LIFE.

Mahatma Gandhi

True happiness comes from the joy of deeds well done, the zest of creating things new.

Antoine de Saint-Exupéry

Be yourself. The world worships the original.

Ingrid Bergman

**Carry laughter
with you wherever
you go.**

Hugh Sidey

He has achieved success who has lived well, laughed often, and loved much.

Bessie Anderson Stanley

'Tis better to have
loved and lost
than never to have
loved at all.

Alfred, Lord Tennyson

Do your little bit of good where you are; it's those little bits of good put together that overwhelm the world.

Desmond Tutu

The limits of the
possible can only
be defined by going
beyond them into
the impossible.

Arthur C. Clarke

I think that beauty comes from being happy and connected to the people we love.

Marcia Cross

The Eskimo has fifty-two names for snow because it is important to them; there ought to be as many for love.

Margaret Atwood

THROW CAUTION TO THE WIND AND JUST DO IT.

Carrie Underwood

**Do not dwell
in the past,
do not dream
of the future,
concentrate the
mind on the
present moment.**

Buddhist saying

**The human race
has only one
really effective
weapon, and that
is laughter.**

Mark Twain

Love is
the magician
that pulls
man out of
his own hat.

Ben Hecht

Wherever you
go, go with all
your heart.

Confucius

What does love feel like? Incredible.

Rebecca Adlington

Laughter is the shortest distance between two people.

Victor Borge

You can, you should, and if you're brave enough to start, you will.

Stephen King

When you're true to who you are, amazing things happen.

Deborah Norville

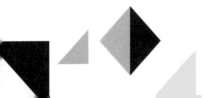

FOLLOW YOUR OWN STAR.

Dante Alighieri

The way to know
life is to love
many things.

Vincent Van Gogh

Love is the enchanted dawn of every heart.

Alphonse de Lamartine

I'd far rather be happy than right any day.

Douglas Adams

Our soulmate is the one who makes life come to life.

Richard Bach

Laugh, and the world laughs with you.

Ella Wheeler Wilcox

WE CAN ONLY LEARN TO LOVE BY LOVING.

Iris Murdoch

Life is a helluva lot more fun if you say 'yes' rather than 'no'.

Richard Branson

Love is
everything it's
cracked up to be...
~~it really is worth~~
fighting for, being
brave for, risking
everything for.

Erica Jong

LIFE IS THE FLOWER FOR WHICH LOVE IS THE HONEY.

Victor Hugo

In dreams and in love there are no impossibilities.

János Arany

Lose not yourself
in a far off time,
seize the moment
that is thine.

Friedrich Schiller

Why not just live
in the moment,
especially if it
has a good beat?

Goldie Hawn

YOU NEVER LOSE BY LOVING.

Barbara De Angelis

Everything in our life should be based on love.

Ray Bradbury

To thine own self be true.

William Shakespeare

Think big thoughts but relish small pleasures.

H. Jackson Brown Jr

What the world really needs is more love and less paperwork.

Pearl Bailey

Life is either a daring adventure or nothing.

Helen Keller

The best thing to hold on to in life is each other.

Audrey Hepburn

You only get
one chance at life
and you have to
grab it boldly.

Bear Grylls

Love is not blind.
It is an extra eye,
which shows us what
is most worthy
of regard.

J. M. Barrie

Why did we wait for anything? – why not seize the pleasure at once?

Jane Austen

LIVE SIMPLY.
DREAM BIG.
BE GRATEFUL.
GIVE LOVE.
LAUGH LOTS.

Anonymous

At the height
of laughter,
the universe
is flung into a
kaleidoscope of
new possibilities.

Jean Houston

Into the house where joy lives, happiness will gladly come.

Japanese proverb

There is no instinct like the heart.

Lord Byron

Go after your dreams, don't be afraid to push the boundaries. And laugh a lot - it's good for you!

Paula Radcliffe

**Every day holds
the possibility of
a miracle.**

Elizabeth David

A heart that loves is always young.

Greek proverb

If my mind can conceive it, and my heart can believe it, I know I can achieve it.

Jesse Jackson

The love we give away is the only love we keep.

Elbert Hubbard

A GOOD LAUGH IS SUNSHINE IN A HOUSE.

William Makepeace Thackeray

Love is composed
of a single
soul inhabiting
two bodies.

Aristotle

Be faithful to
that which
exists within
yourself.

 André Gide

Nothing shows
a man's character
more than what
he laughs at.

Johann Wolfgang von Goethe

May you live every day of your life.

Jonathan Swift

What force is more potent than love?

Igor Stravinsky

ENTHUSIASM MOVES THE WORLD.

Arthur Balfour

Always be a first-rate version of yourself, instead of a second-rate version of somebody else.

Judy Garland

One way to get the
most out of life is
to look upon it as
an adventure.

William Feather

THERE ARE NO TRAFFIC JAMS ALONG THE EXTRA MILE.

Roger Staubach

Love is a canvas furnished by nature and embroidered by imagination.

Voltaire

Love is like smiling; it never fades and is contagious.

Anonymous

To love and
be loved is to
feel the sun from
both sides.

David Viscott

LAUGHTER TO ME IS BEING ALIVE.

William Saroyan

Dwell on the beauty of life. Watch the stars, and see yourself running with them.

Marcus Aurelius

Happiness is a way of travel, not a destination.

Roy M. Goodman

First say to yourself what you would be; and then do what you have to do.

Epictetus

If we all did the things we are capable of, we would literally astound ourselves.

Thomas Edison

The future depends on what you do today.

Mahatma Gandhi

Have a heart that never hardens, and a temper that never tires, and a touch that never hurts.

Charles Dickens

Dream as if you'll live forever. Live as if you'll die today.

James Dean

It is never too late to be what you might have been.

Adelaide Anne Procter

The purpose
of dancing – and
of life – is to enjoy
every moment and
every step.

Wayne W. Dyer

THE GREATEST PLEASURE OF LIFE IS LOVE.

Euripides

Tell me who admires and loves you, and I will tell you who you are.

Antoine de Saint-Exupéry

Be yourself; everyone else is already taken.

Oscar Wilde

Life is short. Kiss slowly, laugh insanely, love truly and forgive quickly.

Paulo Coelho

Nothing to me feels
as good as laughing
incredibly hard.

Steve Carell

Wrinkles should merely indicate where the smiles have been.

Mark Twain

Love is like
pi – natural,
irrational,
and very
important.

Lisa Hoffman

Don't count the days; make the days count.

Anonymous

The only reason to be alive is to enjoy it.

Rita Mae Brown

LOVE IS A GAME THAT TWO CAN PLAY AND BOTH WIN.

Eva Gabor

Act as if what
you do makes
a difference.
It does.

William James

Love is the
bee that
carries the
pollen from
one heart
to another.

Slash Coleman

If you have good thoughts they will shine out of your face like sunbeams and you will always look lovely.

Roald Dahl

Enjoy the little things, for one day you may look back and realise they were the big things.

Robert Brault

We build
too many
walls and
not enough
bridges.

Isaac Newton

DON'T WAIT. THE TIME WILL NEVER BE JUST RIGHT.

Napoleon Hill

I honestly think
it's the thing
I like most, to
laugh. It cures a
multitude of ills.

Audrey Hepburn

Life is not measured
by the number of
breaths you take,
but by the moments
that take your
breath away.

Anonymous

LOVE LOVES TO LOVE LOVE.

James Joyce

Try to be like the turtle – at ease in your own shell.

Bill Copeland

Do something wonderful; people may imitate it.

Albert Schweitzer

There is only
one happiness in
life: to love and
be loved.

George Sand

THE THINGS THAT WE LOVE TELL US WHAT WE ARE.

Thomas Aquinas

Always do what is right. It will gratify half of mankind and astound the other.

Mark Twain

Every
moment
is a fresh
beginning.

T. S. Eliot

There is nothing in the world so irresistibly contagious as laughter and good humour.

Charles Dickens

Always laugh when you can. It is cheap medicine.

Lord Byron

The man that loves and laughs must sure do well.

Alexander Pope

Leave something
for someone
but don't leave
someone for
something.

Enid Blyton

Go as far as you
can see; when you
get there, you'll be
able to see further.

Thomas Carlyle

Give out what you most want to come back.

Robin Sharma

Your attitude is like
a box of crayons that
colour your world.

Allen Klein

WHATEVER YOU ARE, BE A GOOD ONE.

William Makepeace Thackeray

Don't save things for a special occasion. Every day of your life is a special occasion.

Anonymous

**The madness
of love is
the greatest
of heaven's
blessings.**

Plato

Who, being loved, is poor?

Oscar Wilde

Whatever you can do
or dream you can,
begin it. Boldness
has genius, power
and magic in it.

Johann Wolfgang von Goethe

LOVE CONQUERS ALL.

Virgil

If you love life,
life will love
you back.

Arthur Rubinstein

Being deeply
loved by someone
gives you strength,
while loving
someone deeply
gives you courage.

Lao Tzu

Do anything, but let it produce joy.

Henry Miller

BEGIN, BE BOLD AND VENTURE TO BE WISE.

Horace

Do not wait to strike till the iron is hot; but make it hot by striking.

W. B. Yeats

To love is to receive a glimpse of heaven.

Karen Sunde

If you are ever
in doubt as to
whether or not you
should kiss a pretty
girl, always give
her the benefit of
the doubt.

Thomas Carlyle

**Sometimes the
heart sees what
is invisible to
the eye.**

H. Jackson Brown Jr

Believe and act as if it were impossible to fail.

Charles Kettering

TRUE LOVE STORIES NEVER HAVE ENDINGS.

Richard Bach

The most wasted of all days is that in which we have not laughed.

Nicolas Chamfort

Be happy with what
you have and are,
be generous with
both, and you won't
have to hunt
for happiness.

William Gladstone

THE MORE WE DO, THE MORE WE CAN DO.

William Hazlitt

What soap is to the body, laughter is to the soul.

Yiddish proverb

Those who bring sunshine into the lives of others cannot keep it from themselves.

J. M. Barrie

As soon as
you start to
pursue a dream,
your life wakes
up and everything
has meaning.

Barbara Sher

I THINK TO LOVE BRAVELY IS THE BEST.

Marilyn Monroe

If opportunity doesn't knock, build a door.

Milton Berle

Laughter is a sunbeam of the soul.

Thomas Mann

**Rise to the occasion,
which is life.**

Virginia Euwer Wolff

Do all things with love.

Og Mandino

If you're interested in finding out more about our books, find us on Facebook at Summersdale Publishers and follow us on Twitter at @Summersdale.

www.summersdale.com